# Dora's WIZZLE WORLD ADVENTURE

adapted by Leigh Olsen
based on the screenplay "Dora's Big Birthday Adventure"
written by Valerie Walsh Valdes
illustrated by Victoria Miller

Ready-to-Read

Simon Spotlight/Nickelodeon
New York    London    Toronto    Sydney

Based on the TV series *Dora the Explorer*™ as seen on Nick Jr.™

SIMON SPOTLIGHT
An imprint of Simon & Schuster Children's Publishing Division
1230 Avenue of the Americas, New York, New York 10020
© 2010 Viacom International Inc. NICKELODEON, NICK JR., *Dora the Explorer*, and all related
titles, logos, and characters are trademarks of Viacom International Inc.
All rights reserved, including the right of reproduction in whole or in part in any form.
SIMON SPOTLIGHT, READY-TO-READ, and colophon are registered trademarks of
Simon & Schuster, Inc.
For information about special discounts for bulk purchases, please contact Simon & Schuster
Special Sales at 1-866-506-1949 or business@simonandschuster.com.
Manufactured in the United States of America 0711 LAK
6 8 10 9 7 5
Library of Congress Cataloging-in-Publication Data
Olsen, Leigh.
Dora's wizzle world adventure / adapted by Leigh Olsen. — 1st ed.
p. cm. — (Ready-to-read)
"Based on the screenplay 'Dora's Big Birthday Adventure' written by Valerie Walsh Valdes."
"Based on the TV series Dora the Explorer as seen on Nick Jr."—T.p. verso.
ISBN 978-1-4424-0353-6
I. Dora the Explorer (Television program) II. Title.
PZ7.O51762Do 2010
[E]—dc22
2009042650

Hi! I am .
DORA

This is my friend .
BOOTS

We are in Wizzle World.

Our friends the 
WIZZLES

live here.

But we have to go  .
HOME

Today is my birthday!

I am having a party.

My friends and family

are waiting for me.

You are invited too!

First we have to find

the .

WISHING WIZZLE

We need to give him

the Wishing ⬡.

CRYSTAL

Then he can wish us 🏠 !

HOME

But there is a mean  .

WITCH

She does not like wishes.

She will try to stop us.

We have to be careful!

"We're off to see the 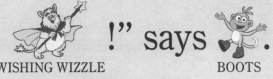 !" says  .

WISHING WIZZLE          BOOTS

The 🦔🦔 wave good-bye.

WIZZLES

"Good luck!" they say.

But how do we find the  ?

WISHING WIZZLE

Let's ask  .

MAP

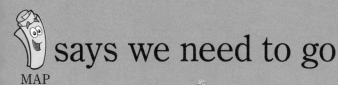 says we need to go

across ,

SEA SNAKE LAKE

through the 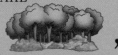,

DANCING FOREST

and over the .

RAINBOW

Do you see ?
SEA SNAKE LAKE

There it is!

But oh, no!

There is a big .
SEA SNAKE

How will we get across?

Look! A Wizzle !
BUBBLE

 and I can get inside.
BOOTS

Then we can float

over .
SEA SNAKE LAKE

Watch out!

The  is here!

WITCH

She has a 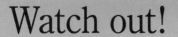 !

MAGIC WAND

She uses it to zap holes

in our Wizzle ◯ !

BUBBLE

 has

**BACKPACK**

some sticky .

**TAPE**

 tapes up the holes.

**BOOTS**

Hooray! We got to the

other side of  !

**SEA SNAKE LAKE**

Next we need to go through

the .

DANCING FOREST

But the

DANCING TREES

won't let us through

unless we dance!

You can help us!
Will you wiggle
from side to side?
Good job!
We made it through
the  DANCING FOREST !

Now we have to go

over the .
RAINBOW

A 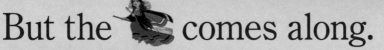 takes us across!
UNICORN

But the  comes along.
WITCH

She makes it 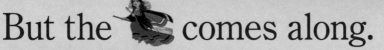.
RAIN

The  is fading away!
RAINBOW

We say, ",
go away!
Come again another day!"
It stops raining, and we
cross the .
RAINBOW

Yay! We made it to the .

We give him the Wishing .

The  is angry.
WITCH

She points her
MAGIC WAND

and breaks the .
CRYSTAL

What will we do?

Will the ⬡ still work?
CRYSTAL

The
WISHING WIZZLE

tells me to wish for
HOME

and think of my friends

and family.

"I wish to go

back ,"  I say.
HOME

I think of  ,
BENNY

, , and . 
ISA  TICO  DIEGO

I think of , ,
MAMI  PAPI

, and the .
ABUELA  TWINS

I think of everyone I know!

The works!
CRYSTAL

BOOTS and I

are at my party.

All of my friends

and family are here.

Everyone gives me

a big hug.

"Happy birthday,  DORA !"
they say.

I am so happy
to see everyone again!
Thank you for helping
me get back  !
HOME